Flora's Magic House

Written and Illustrated by Binette Schroeder

North-South Books
New York London Toronto Melbourne

First published under the title *Lupinchen* in the United States in 1969
by Seymour Lawrence and in Great Britain in 1969 by Macdonald & Co.
(Publishers) Ltd. and reissued for the United States, Great Britain,
Canada, Australia and New Zealand in 1986 by North-South Books, an
imprint of Rada Matija AG.

Distributed in the United States by
Holt, Rinehart and Winston, 383 Madison Avenue,
New York, New York, 10017.
Library of Congress Catalog Card Number 85-63299

ISBN 0-03-008024-X

Distributed in Great Britain by
Blackie and Son Ltd, Furnival House, 14–18 High Holborn,
London WC1V 6BX.
British Library Cataloguing in Publication Data

Schroeder, Binette
  Flora's magic house.
  I. Title   II. Lupinchen. *English*
  823'.914[J]   PZ7

ISBN 0-200-72886-5

Distributed in Canada by
Douglas & McIntyre Ltd., Toronto.
Canadian Cataloguing in Publication Data available in
Marc Record from National Library of Canada.
ISBN 0 88894 772 0

Distributed in Australia and New Zealand by
Buttercup Books Pty. Ltd., Melbourne.
ISBN 0 949447 24 2

Printed in Germany

For Els and Ursuline

Once upon a time, in a magic land of trees and flowers and misty clouds, a doll named Flora lived in a garden with her friend Robert the Bird. Every day, while Flora planted new seedlings and watered her flowers, Robert the Bird flew about collecting grapes, gooseberries, cherries and other good things to eat. They were very happy together, but sometimes Flora wondered what else there was to see and do in the world outside.

"You're lucky," she said to Robert the Bird. "You have wings and can fly away over the fields and out across the sea. I have to stay here all alone."

Robert the Bird understood that she was lonely, so he invited two friends to visit them. Humpty Dumpty was a quiet fellow with a top hat and an umbrella. Magic Box was a show-off. He smiled, gave a deep bow, and underneath his lid Flora saw a splendid flower.

"Where did you pick that?" she asked.

"I made it," said Magic Box. "I can make anything!"

Robert the Bird had work to do and flew away, leaving them to amuse themselves.

"What else can you make besides a flower?" asked Flora.

"Anything you like," said Magic Box. "What about a paper house?"

"Oh, yes!" said Flora.

Magic Box quickly unrolled some long strips of paper. "One, two, three," he counted, with a flourish of his scissors. Then, with a snip here and a snip there, a house began to take shape. Flora stared at him, fascinated.

"There you are, Flora," said Magic Box, as he proudly led her into the paper house. "Now watch!" He reached beneath his lid and started to bring out all sorts of tempting things to eat. There was ice cream (strawberry, raspberry and vanilla), a chocolate cake, a cherry tart, a pot of cocoa, a bowl of whipped cream and a great fistful of lollipops.

Meanwhile Humpty Dumpty had climbed upstairs and stuck his head out of the chimney. "Oh, dear," he said. "Listen to the wind blowing through the trees." But the others didn't want to listen.

"Come and have some cocoa," called Flora.

When every crumb of cake had disappeared and the last lollipop had been licked down to its stick, the house suddenly started to quiver. "What was that?" asked Flora uneasily.

"Only a puff of wind," said Magic Box. "Nothing to worry about."

But the house shook more and more, and soon they all got a peculiar floating feeling. As Flora peered through the window, the paper house lifted off the ground, the flowers dropped away out of sight, and she found herself staring down at the tops of the trees. "We're blowing away!" she cried in alarm. "What can we do?"

Humpty Dumpty thought very hard for a moment. "What we ought to do," he said, "is to put wings on our house. Then it will be an airplane." Taking Magic Box's scissors, he calmly snipped away as the wind whistled past. Very soon the job was done.

Magic Box seemed quite unable to help. Earlier he had strutted around the cabin, but now the sight of the ground whirling past filled him with terror. "I'm only paper," he thought. "I might easily blow away."

As the airplane climbed and dipped and twisted, Magic Box began to look rather green.

Flora, her hair streaming in the wind, shouted "hello" to Claudia Cat in a tree far below. Claudia Cat was so surprised that she almost fell off her branch.

They glided on over the fields. "Look at the cows," shouted Flora. "Their tails are blowing in the wind."

Suddenly she saw the sea. "Oh, how beautiful," she cried. "What fun it is to fly!"

But then the picnic things began to rattle. The airplane gave a great lurch and everything slid off the table.

"Prepare for an emergency landing!" shouted Humpty Dumpty as they were all thrown off their feet. "The wind has dropped. We are coming down in ——" A loud splash interrupted him.

Humpty Dumpty looked at the frightened faces of the others. "If we are in the water, what we need is a boat," he said. "I must see what I can do." Once again he borrowed Magic Box's scissors and the airplane was swiftly turned into a splendid boat.

"But paper will get wet and sink," moaned Flora.

Magic Box knew she was right, so he climbed to the top of the boat and hung on for dear life. Then Flora started throwing all the furniture and the cups and plates into the sea to lighten the boat.

Humpty Dumpty kept bailing with his top hat. "Don't throw away my umbrella!" he said. "You never know when it may come in useful." Still, the paper boat sank lower and lower in the icy water.

"Abandon ship!" cried Humpty Dumpty. "Launch the umbrella!" Flora quickly unfurled it. They tumbled in, Flora sitting on top of Humpty Dumpty's head. Magic Box, who was light as a feather, jumped in terror onto Flora's shoulders and held onto her hair.

Humpty Dumpty tried to think how he could steer their floating umbrella to land. They were all very quiet. Flora was wondering if adventures were such fun after all.

Suddenly, as the bow of the paper boat disappeared beneath the waves, Magic Box gave a little shriek. The others trembled as a huge shadow swept over them with a sound like rushing wind. What could it be?

It was Robert the Bird! "Dear Robert!" exclaimed Flora. "How did you find us?"

Robert the Bird helped them climb out of the floating umbrella onto his back. "The garden was empty without you, Flora," he said. "The flowers lost all their perfume; you took it with you. I simply followed your scent — and here I am."

As dusk fell, Robert the Bird flew up into the sky. Beating the air gently with his wings, so that the three tired wanderers would not fall off, he headed for home.

Flora sighed with relief once they were safely back in the garden. Humpty Dumpty, in his soaking top hat, still wore a worried expression. Magic Box felt rather ashamed of himself. The three of them had nearly drowned because of his boasting.

"Drink your tea," said Robert the Bird, noticing their sleepy eyes.

Later, Flora watched her two new friends walk off through the purple darkness. "That was fun," she said to Robert the Bird, "but it's good to be back." Then she leaned comfortably against his soft, warm feathers.

Soon they were both asleep, and once more everything in the garden lay quiet and peaceful under the watchful eye of the moon.